A Crabtree Branches Book

EXTREME SPORTS

Motocross

Bernard Conaghan

Crabtree Publishing
crabtreebooks.com

School-to-Home Support for Caregivers and Teachers

This high-interest book is designed to motivate striving students with engaging topics while building fluency, vocabulary, and an interest in reading. Here are a few questions and activities to help the reader build upon his or her comprehension skills.

Before Reading:

- *What do I think this book is about?*
- *What do I know about this topic?*
- *What do I want to learn about this topic?*
- *Why am I reading this book?*

During Reading:

- *I wonder why...*
- *I'm curious to know...*
- *How is this like something I already know?*
- *What have I learned so far?*

After Reading:

- *What was the author trying to teach me?*
- *What are some details?*
- *How did the photographs and captions help me understand more?*
- *Read the book again and look for the vocabulary words.*
- *What questions do I still have?*

Extension Activities:

- *What was your favorite part of the book? Write a paragraph on it.*
- *Draw a picture of your favorite thing you learned from the book.*

Table of Contents

What Is Motocross?

Motocross is an **extreme** bike sport. Racers zip around the course on motorcycles known as dirt bikes. The **terrain** of the course is often a rough track made of dirt, gravel, or mud. The first known motocross race took place in the United Kingdom in 1924.

Fun Fact

Motocross got its name from combining "cross country" with *motocyclette*, which is the French word for motorcycle.

Motocross in Action

Motocross is one of the most popular extreme sports in the world. There are different types of motocross.

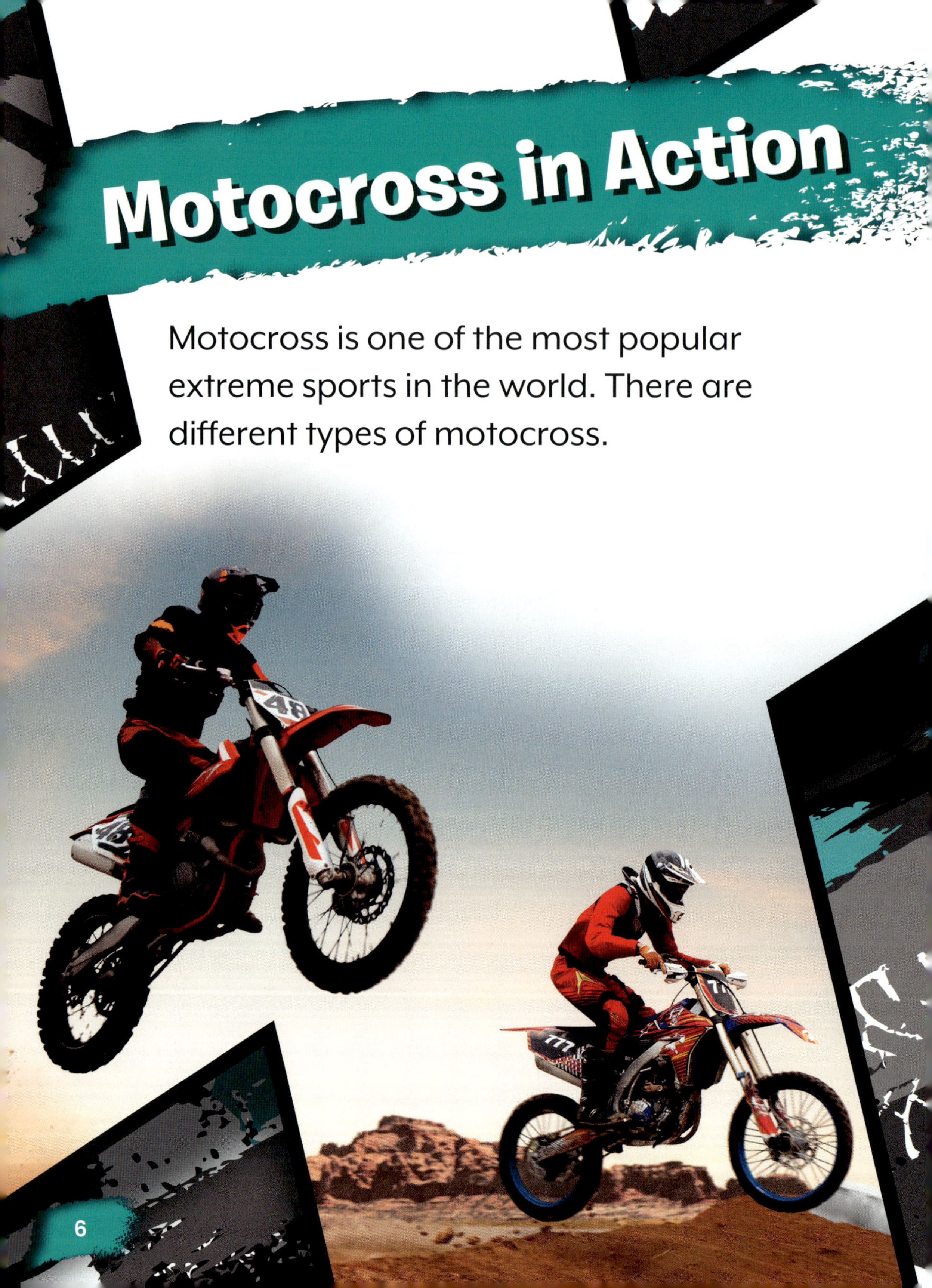

Fun Fact

Most motocross tracks can have 25 to 30 riders per race.

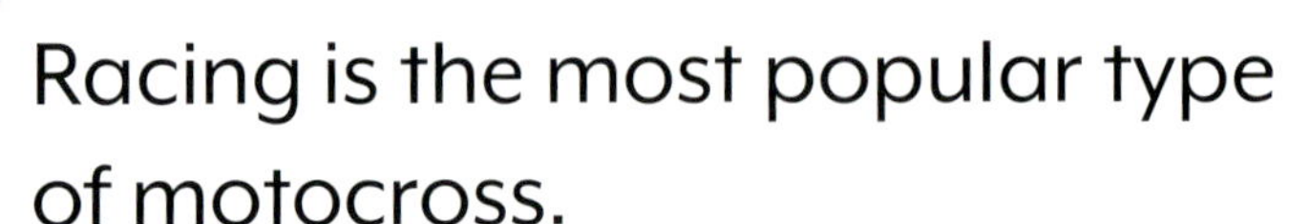

Racing is the most popular type of motocross.

Fun Fact

A motocross race is made up of two races, called motos.

Tracks are 1 to 3 miles (1.6 to 4.8 km) long. Before a race, riders will often walk the course and do a practice ride to get to know the track.

Freestyle motocross is when riders perform different types of tricks. It is also known as FMX. Instead of focusing on speed, riders perform tricks and stunts. These can include jumps, as well as midair spins and flips.

Fun Fact

Freestyle motocross legend Travis Pastrana invented the cliffhanger.

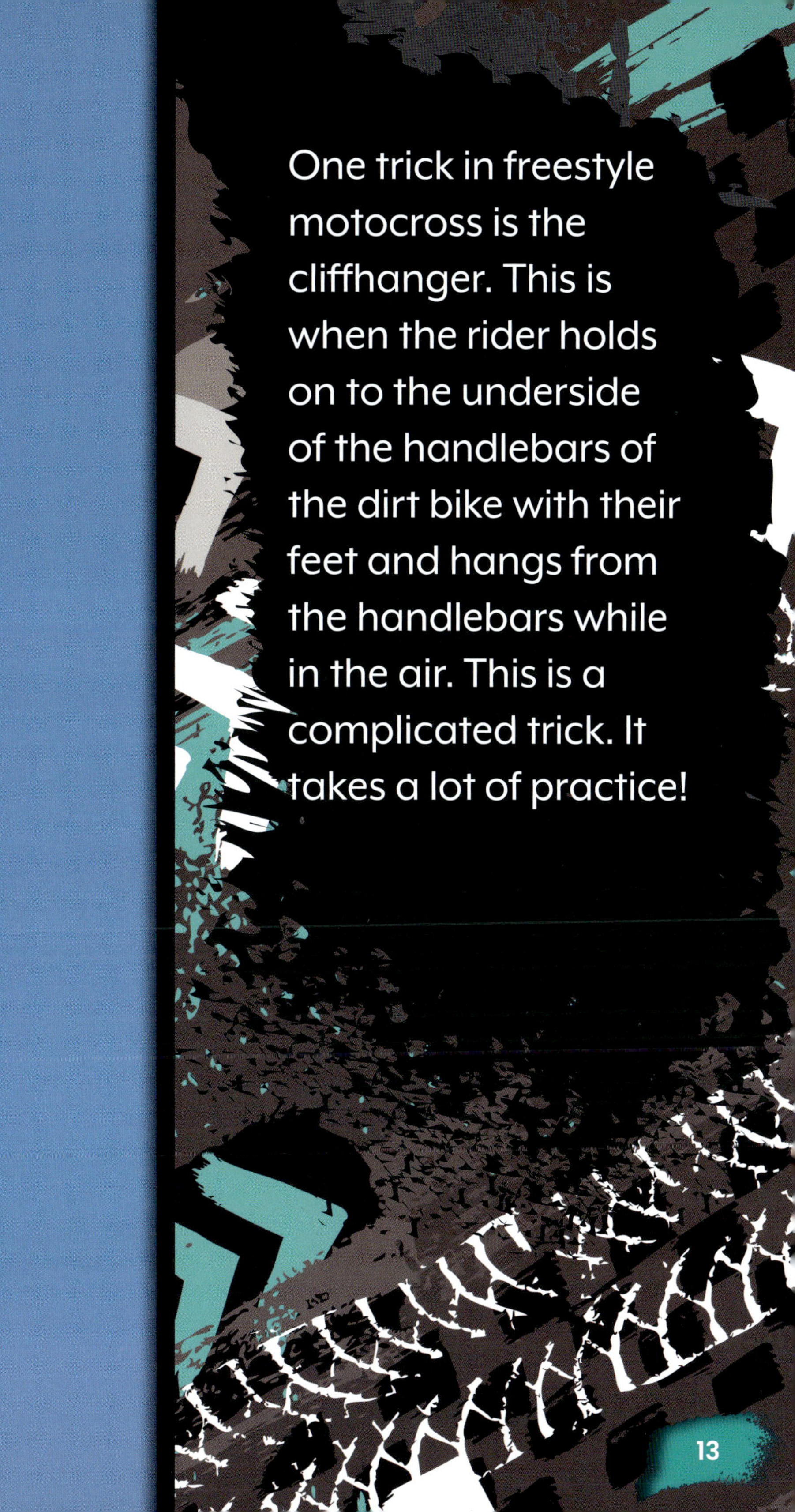

One trick in freestyle motocross is the cliffhanger. This is when the rider holds on to the underside of the handlebars of the dirt bike with their feet and hangs from the handlebars while in the air. This is a complicated trick. It takes a lot of practice!

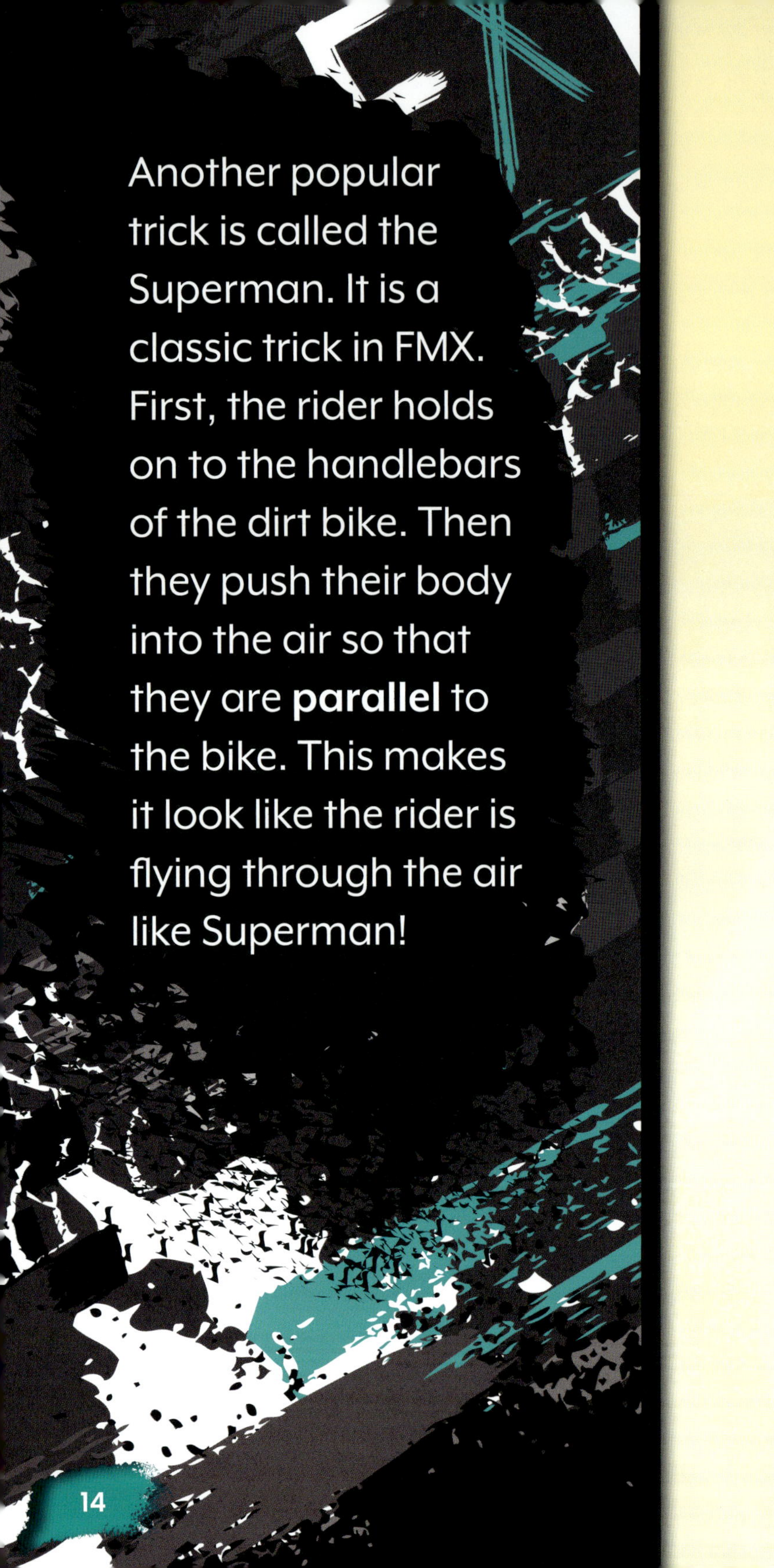

Another popular trick is called the Superman. It is a classic trick in FMX. First, the rider holds on to the handlebars of the dirt bike. Then they push their body into the air so that they are **parallel** to the bike. This makes it look like the rider is flying through the air like Superman!

The ruler is also a popular FMX trick. To do this trick, the rider holds on to the handlebars and throws their feet straight up into the air, keeping their body perfectly lined up with their dirt bike. The rider tries to be as straight as possible, to look like a ruler. This is an extremely complicated trick. It takes a lot of practice to master.

Parts of a Dirt Bike

The most important part of a dirt bike is the **chassis**. It is the **frame** of the bike. The chassis is made of aluminum or steel. The **axle** is where the wheels on the bike connect to the chassis. The tires are specially made for the rough terrain of motocross.

The engine of a dirt bike is what gives it power and makes it go. It is in the center of the frame.

Fun Fact

The first motorcycle was created in France in the 1860s.

There are two types of dirt bike engines: the two-stroke and the four-stroke. The two-stroke engine has more power, but the four-stroke is more **durable**.

Your Motocross Career

The best way to start competing in motocross is to go out on the track and start practicing. A coach can teach you the basics of the sport. They can also help you improve your tricks.

27
MARZOCCHI

Fun Fact

Sports in the X Games include motocross, skateboarding, skiing, and snowboarding.

If you become a good motocross rider, you might be able to compete in the X Games or other **tournaments**. The X Games is an extreme sports event held twice a year, in the winter and the summer.

Motocross Legends

Motocross has a variety of legends. One of them is Ricky Carmichael. He has won seven AMA Motocross Championships. He was born on November 27, 1979, in Clearwater, Florida.

thor

Another legend is Ashley Fiolek. Born on October 22, 1990, Fiolek has won many motocross awards and helped change the sport of motocross for women. She competed in the AMA Motocross Championships from 2008 to 2012, and is a four-time AMA women's motocross national champion.

Fun Fact

Fiolek has been deaf since birth.

Glossary

axle (AK·sl): A bar on which a wheel turns

chassis (CHASS·ee): The supporting frame of a motor vehicle

durable (DOOR_uh-buhl): Something that stays strong and in good condition for a long period of time

extreme (ek·STREEM): Something that is far beyond the normal

frame (FRAYM): The structure or shape of something

freestyle (FREE·stile): In sports, a performance or competition in which participants are allowed to use different styles or methods

legend (LEH·jind): Someone who is famous and admired for doing something well

parallel (PEH·ruh·lel): Lines that move in the same direction, that are the same distance apart for their whole length, and that do not touch

terrain (ter·AYN): An area of land

tournament (TUR·nuh·ment): A competition with many participants

Index

Websites to Visit

www.redbull.com/us-en/how-to-get-into-motocross

www.xgames.com

https://americanmotorcyclist.com

About the Author

Bernard Conaghan lives in South Carolina with his German shepherd named Duke. Every year he goes snowboarding in Switzerland. He is a coach on his son's football team. He always eats one scoop of peach ice cream after dinner.

Written by: Bernard Conaghan
Designed by: Jen Bowers
Series Development: James Earley
Proofreader: Melissa Boyce
Educational Consultant: Marie Lemke M.Ed.

Photographs: Cover image ©2018 Artur Didyk/Shutterstock, background ©Matisson_ART/Shutterstock; p.3 ©2012 PhilipYb Studio/Shutterstock; p.5 ©2017 Artur Didyk/Shutterstock; p.6 ©2019 Artur Didyk/Shutterstock; p.7 ©2021 Steam visuals/Shutterstock, phone ©2017 Vasin Lee/Shutterstock; p.8 ©2012 PhilipYb Studio/Shutterstock; p.9 ©2019 Todor Stoyanov/Shutterstock; p.11 ©2018 Artur Didyk/Shutterstock; p.12 ©2021 Yurchenko S/Shutterstock; p.15 ©2018 Flystock/Shutterstock; p.16 ©2020 Miloserdovart/Shutterstock; p.18 ©2016 Suvorov_Alex/Shutterstock; p.19 ©2020 PIPAT YAPATHANASAP/Shutterstock; p.20 ©2007 Margo Harrison/Shutterstock; p.21 ©2009 Warren Price Photography/Shutterstock; p.22 ©2021 Nasrul Ma Arif/Shutterstock; p.23 ©2011 Pukhov K/Shutterstock; p.24 ©2011 Juan Camilo Bernal/Shutterstock, medals © Net Vector/Shutterstock; p.26 ©2008 Philipe Ancheta/Shutterstock; p.27 By cole24_/CC BY-SA 2.0/https://www.flickr.com/photos/racecarphotos/524115850; p.28 ©2012 Kathy Hutchins/Shutterstock; p.29 ©2010 Warren Price Photography/Shutterstock

Crabtree Publishing

crabtreebooks.com 800-387-7650

Printed in the U.S.A./012023/CG20220815

Published in Canada
Crabtree Publishing
616 Welland Avenue
St. Catharines, Ontario
L2M 5V6

Published in the United States
Crabtree Publishing
347 Fifth Avenue
Suite 1402-145
New York, New York 10016

Library and Archives Canada Cataloguing in Publication
Available at Library and Archives Canada

Library of Congress Cataloging-in-Publication Data
Available at the Library of Congress

Hardcover: 978-1-0396-9663-1
Paperback: 978-1-0396-9770-6
Ebook (pdf): 978-1-0396-9984-7
Epub: 978-1-0396-9877-2